The Journey of
OLIVER K. WOODMAN

The Journey of

WRITTEN BY **Darcy Pattison**

ILLUSTRATED BY **Joe Cepeda**

OLIVER K. WOODMAN

Harcourt, Inc.

San Diego   New York   London

Library of Congress Cataloging-in-Publication Data
Pattison, Darcy.
The journey of Oliver K. Woodman/Darcy Pattison;
illustrated by Joe Cepeda.
p.   cm.
Summary: Oliver K. Woodman, a man made of wood, takes a remarkable
journey across America, as told through the postcards and letters of those
he meets along the way.
[1. Dolls—Fiction.   2. Travel—Fiction.   3. Postcards—Fiction.
4. Letters—Fiction.]   I. Cepeda, Joe, ill.   II. Title.
PZ7.P27816Jo   2003
[E]—dc21   2001005320
ISBN 0-15-202329-1

First edition
H G F E D C B A

Printed in Singapore

The paintings in this book were done in oils over an acrylic under-painting on board.
The display type was set in OPTI Publicity Gothic and Typewriter.
Color separations by Bright Arts Ltd., Hong Kong
Printed and bound by Tien Wah Press, Singapore
This book was printed on totally chlorine-free Enso Stora Matte paper.
Production supervision by Sandra Grebenar and Pascha Gerlinger
Designed by Lydia D'moch

For Dwight
—D. P.

For that seventeen-year-old boy
with an undaunted spirit of adventure,
who left home twenty-five years ago
and faced the world
—J. C.

May 17
Rock Hill, SC

Dear Tameka,
    I'd love to come to California,
but I can't. I will be building
kitchen cabinets for some
new apartments all summer.
    But maybe my friend Oliver
will come to visit!

Love,
Uncle Ray

Dear Traveler,

I am going to see Tameka Schwartz, 370 Park Avenue, Redcrest, California, 95569. Please give me a ride and help me get there. If you don't mind, drop a note to my friend Raymond Johnson, 111 Stony Lane, Rock Hill, South Carolina, 29730. He wants to keep up with my travels.

Thanks,
OLIVER K. WOODMAN

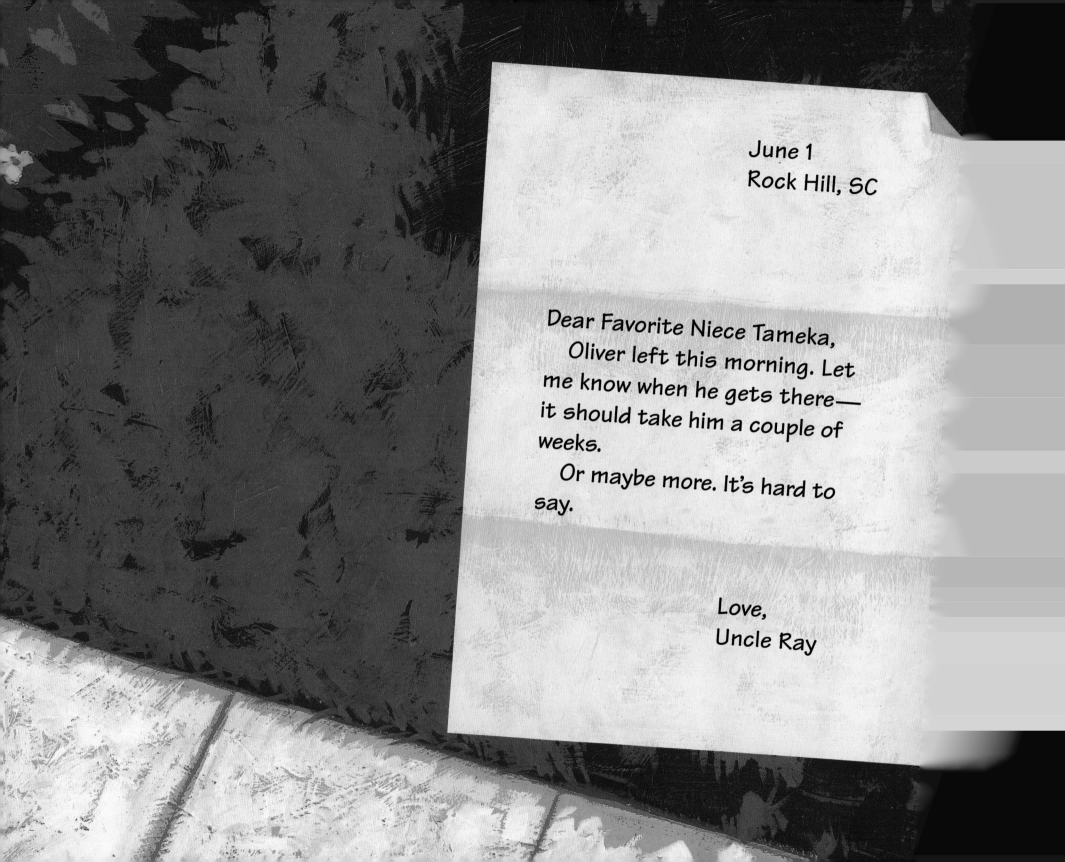

June 1
Rock Hill, SC

Dear Favorite Niece Tameka,
    Oliver left this morning. Let me know when he gets there— it should take him a couple of weeks.
    Or maybe more. It's hard to say.

Love,
Uncle Ray

June 4
McTavish Plantation
Outside Memphis, Tennessee

Dear Ray:
For two days, Oliver rode in the back of my truck and kept Bert, my Brahman bull, company. I delivered Bert to his new home and he's settling in, but he'll miss the late-night conversations and singing with Oliver.
I left Oliver east of the Mississippi River, just outside Memphis, and hurried home to my beloved Amelia.

Yours truly,
Jackson McTavish

June 8
Forrest City, AR

Hi! Mr. OK is OK. Quinn and Sherry went to a basketball game at The Pyramid in Memphis, Tennessee, last weekend and brought Mr. OK back. He hung out with us for a couple of days, and all the girls liked him better than Quinn. So when Quinn's cousin's boyfriend's aunt was leaving to visit her sick grandfather in Fort Smith, Arkansas, the guys loaded Mr. OK into the aunt's station wagon and sent him on his way. We didn't even get to say good-bye!

Cherry (Sherry's sister),
for the Gang

P.S. If you see Mr. OK again, tell him we all said good-bye.

Raymond Johnson
111 Stony Lane
Rock Hill, SC 29730

June 11
Albuquerque, NM

Hey, Ray—
    I drive a moving van for Southeast
Moving Company. I picked up Oliver at
the Arkansas border, then drove west to
Oklahoma City, Oklahoma, south to Dallas,
Texas, northwest to Amarillo, Texas, east
to Panhandle, Texas, then west again to
Albuquerque, New Mexico. He's an easy
fella to travel with. He never needs
bathroom stops. He doesn't care where we
eat. And he stays awake with me all night.
I'm sorry to see him go, but this week the
company is sending me east, to Wauchula,
Florida.

                    Trucking along—
                    Bobbi Jo

Raymond Johnson
111 Stony Lane
Rock Hill, SC 29730

June 28
Rock Hill, SC

Dear Tameka,
I've had no word from Oliver in seventeen days. I'm starting to worry. What if he is lost?
Please call me if he turns up at your house.

Love,
Uncle Ray

July 1
Redcrest, CA

Dear Uncle Ray,
   No word from Oliver. Are you sure
he's really coming?
   I still wish we could see you. I
asked Mama if we could come visit,
but she said it costs too much.
Daddy says he can't take off work
that long. Ever since I asked, Mama
keeps looking at family photo albums.
When she sees your pictures, she
says, "My baby brother!"
                              Love,

Tameka

XOXOXOX

July 4
Salt Lake City, UT

Dear Raymond Johnson:
　My grandfather found Mr. Woodman in the middle of the reservation in New Mexico. Poor fella—a mouse was building a nest in his backpack. We don't know how he ended up way out there, and he's not telling. Grandpa brought him to Utah to join me in the Fourth of July parade. I got so tired of smiling and waving at the crowds, but Mr. Woodman's brave smile inspired me.
　I just sent Mr. Woodman off with three sisters. They looked like such nice old ladies, so I know they'll take good care of him.

With all my love—
Melissa Tso, Miss Utah

P. S. I've enclosed an autographed picture.

July 27

en route to San Francisco, CA

Dear Mr. Johnson:

My sisters and I had the distinct pleasure of entertaining Mr. Oliver K. Woodman for the past 23 days. You see, we've lived in Kokomo, Indiana, all our lives. Until now, we'd never been west of the Mississippi River. Our dear papa died in January and left us an inheritance. We decided to use the money to tour the West this year. While in Salt Lake City, we saw Mr. Oliver in a parade, and after talking it over, we voted to give him a ride.

We stopped at a rodeo in Eureka, Nevada, where Mr. Oliver met an old friend named Bert. They had a moving reunion. Agnes, my oldest sister, insisted we show Mr. Oliver the great city of Reno. Mr. Oliver's advice was very helpful. We won $5,000!

We are heading south to San Francisco to see the Golden Gate Bridge, so we left Mr. Oliver yesterday in Rough and Ready, California. He should be at Miss Tameka's soon.

The Claremont Sisters

Agnes, Maggie, and Lucinda

P.S. We had afternoon tea every day. Mr. Oliver has the loveliest manners.

July 28
To: Raymond Johnson
Re: Mr. Oliver K. Woodman

Our family, currently on vacation, picked
up the above-named person in what I thought
was a misguided goodwill gesture. Little
did I know how lucky that gesture would be.
Last night, we pitched tents in the
redwood forest. I woke at 3:00 a.m. to
screams of terror. Bears! Your friend
managed to frighten them away. He saved
our lives.
With the deepest and most sincere
gratitude, we intend to deliver him to the
doorstep of Tameka Schwartz within the
next two days.

Gratefully yours,
Bernard Grape, Attorney-at-Law

Raymond Johnson
111 Stony Lane
Rock Hill, SC
29730

August 1
Redcrest, CA

Dear Uncle Ray,
   Guess who came to dinner? Oliver!
   He is so much fun! We are camping in the backyard tonight. I hear he's not scared of anything, so I'm glad he'll be there. Tomorrow, at the river, I'll let him hold my fishing pole while I swim.
   Guess what else? Daddy and Mama talked it over. We're coming to YOUR house next month, and we'll bring Oliver home. Isn't it wonderful?

                                    Love, Tameka
                                    XOXOXOX
P. S. Knock, knock. Who's there? Olive. Olive who? Olive both you and Oliver!

ROCK HILL CITY NEWS
SEPTEMBER 15

TICKER-TAPE PARADE FOR HOMETOWN BOY

by Demetrius Dickson

Oliver K. Woodman will return home today amid national acclaim for his cross-country journey. Woodman began his trip on June 1, in Rock Hill, South Carolina, and arrived in Redcrest, California, on August 1. The Rock Hill City Council announced that a ticker-tape parade to honor Woodman will be held today at 10:00 A.M., starting at the corner of Main Street and Cherry Road and proceeding down Cherry Road to Cherry Park.

Raymond Johnson and Tameka Schwartz, friends of Mr. Woodman, will host a picnic in his honor at Cherry Park at noon. At 1:00 P.M., Mr. Woodman will show postcards and mementos from his trip. The public is invited.